D1203561

The Cheetah

Barney the Bear Killer Series
Book 6

When Dave and I visit schools, I sometimes tell the kids that Barney lives on the farm with all the animals in the Animal Pride Series. When I first wrote the stories about Barney, they were true. But when we put him on the farm with the animals, I added some fiction. So now, the books are half true and half fiction.

We also put our granddaughters on the farm. April, the one Dave calls J.J., (this stands for jabber jaws because she talks all the time) plays me in the Barney the Bear Killer books. Look on the back of Dave's book, **Spike the Black Wolf**, and you will see the girls. April is the blonde. She is a cheerleader. In May, 2004, she graduated from high school.

Look out, boys!

The Cheetah

Barney the Bear Killer Series
Book 6

By Pat L. Sargent

Illustrated by Jane Lenoir

Ozark Publishing, Inc.
P.O. Box 228
Prairie Grove, AR 72753

iii

Cataloging-in-Publication Data

Sargent, Pat, 1936–
    The cheetah / Pat L. Sargent ; illustrated by
Jane Lenoir.—Prairie Grove, AR : Ozark
Publishing, c2005.
      p. cm. (Barney the bear killer series ; 6)

    SUMMARY: A cheetah escapes from a
circus and makes its home on the farm.
When Ashley disappears, Molly takes her
rifle down from the rack on the wall. She
will do whatever it takes to protect her children.
    ISBN 1-56763-973-9 (hb
          1-56763-974-7 (pbk)

    1. Dogs—Juvenile fiction.
[1. Dogs—Fiction. 2. Farm life—Fiction.]
I. Lenoir, Jane, 1950– ill. II. Title. III. Series.

    PZ10.3.S244Ch 2005
    [Fic]—dc20   2003095969

Printed in the United States of America

iv

Inspired by

Brandy Coker and thousands of students across the world who love to read stories and facts about the *fastest* on-land animal.

Dedicated to

Brandy Coker, a third-grade student at Frost Elementary in Frost, Texas. In the spring of 2003, I received a very nice letter from Brandy. She had read some or perhaps all of my books about Barney the Bear Killer and liked them. She suggested the title and the chapter titles for this book. Since the books I write about Barney are half true and half fiction, her idea and suggestion about me writing a book about a cheetah was great. A cheetah did escape from a circus years ago near a town where I lived. So some of the events in this story really happened. Some, of course, are fiction.

Okay, Brandy, this one's for you!
Hope you like it.

Foreword

When a cheetah escapes from a circus and makes its home on the farm, Molly decides it's time to take her rifle down from the rack on the wall. She is carrying an unborn baby in her tummy. She has made up her mind that she will do anything to help protect her five—and soon-to-be six—children, even though the cheetah, over a short distance, is the fastest land animal on earth

Contents

The Cheetah

Barney the Bear Killer Series
Book 6

Barney the Bear Killer Series:
The Grizzly
The Black Panther
The Timber Wolf
Cougar Holler
The Bobcat
The Cheetah

And 10 more coming soon:
Topper, Son of Barney
The Jaguar
The Hungry Lynx
I had written twenty stories about Barney by the time I graduated from high school. They were all true then. But when I put him on the farm with the animals, I added some fiction.

One

Cheetah!

"**G**grrrrrrrrrr!"

Barney's nose began itching and then started twitching, and he felt the hair on the back of his neck stand up. There was something out there, all right. And he knew by the smell that it was coming closer.

Barney had an earache, but there was nothing wrong with his nose. His nose was telling him that there was something in the woods. His eyes began scanning the area. Even though he detected no movement, it didn't matter. It was there.

Pain shot through his left ear. What an earache! If only he could talk. He could tell Farmer John that his ear was hurting, and maybe he would do something about it.

Farmer John turned and looked at Barney, then asked, "Just what was that growling all about, Barney Boy? Is something out there? I saw your eyes on the woods."

Barney the Bear Killer's nose-twitching stopped and the hair on his neck settled down after he planted his strong body on the ground beside his little son.

"Ah, that's what you're doing. You're protecting that young pup, aren't you, boy? I reckon you've already started teaching him the importance of staying on guard, so that he can help protect this family."

Barney's long tongue reached out and licked the little puppy's face. The pup was the spitting image of his daddy. Everything about him was the same, except his size, of course. It was obvious that Barney loved his little son. But then, who wouldn't? He was such a cute little thing.

Their neighbor, Joe Clark, had brought them the pup that afternoon. He had promised that Farmer John could have his pick of the litter for letting Barney be the father of his gyp's pups. He had kept his promise.

The twin boys had been waiting for their turn to pet the little puppy. The three girls had been first in line, starting with Ashley.

A little earlier, when Jake and John began complaining about the girls getting to be first, about the only words that came from Farmer John's mouth were, "It's age before beauty, Boys. Around here, it's always age before beauty." And of course, both boys giggled. Hopefully, they would realize that their daddy was trying to teach them to be polite and always let the ladies go first.

The puppy was looking at the kids. He didn't know what to think. There was only one of those two-legged things at the house where his mama lived. Here, there were five! And they were all arms and legs! They were scary! He looked at his daddy, who was lying there grinning.

"Well," Farmer John said with eyebrows raised. "What are we going to call Barney's new son?"

Names started flying! All five kids began jumping up and down, and each one screamed out a name.

Ashley said, "Let's name him Barney Jr.!"

"That's what I was going to say, Daddy," Amber nodded. "I like that name because he looks like Barney."

April was standing there with thoughts racing through her head. This puppy was special. He needed his own name. Oh, she knew that naming him after his dad might be the thing to do. But even though he was the spitting image of his daddy, she felt like he needed his own name. Someday, he would be *number one*. When Barney went to that big dog heaven in the sky, this black-and-tan puppy would be *uno* (number one).

When Farmer John saw the look on April's face, he skipped her and asked Ashley, "Now what was that name you yelled out, June Bug?"

Ashley smiled mischievously. "I said Barney Jr. but I also like the name Hunter. He'll be a good coon hunter. Barney will teach him everything he knows about coon hunting! Next to Barney, he'll be the best coon dog around when he grows up!"

Farmer John patted the top of Ashley's head and grinned. She was right about this pup. Barney would train his little son right.

"My dad was a sergeant in the army. A first sergeant," Molly said. "Daddy's nickname was Topper. Let's call the new puppy Topper!

When Barney gets old, this puppy will be *top dog*!"

All eyes turned toward Molly. "That's a good name," they said.

That's when another growl escaped Barney's throat. The hair on his back and the back of his neck started rising.

Ole Barney was standing, half crouched, with his eyes glued to the bushes along the edge of the trees.

"What's wrong with you, Boy?" Farmer John asked. "You got a pain in your getalongs? Did you eat too much rabbit, and you've got a tummy ache? Tell me, and I'll try to fix it."

Barney calmed down. He shook his head and his long ears flopped from side to side. He put his left hind foot to his head and scratched his ear.

"Oh, I get it," Farmer John said with a frown. "It's your ear. It hurts. Right?"

Barney the Bear Killer knew that his master finally understood. He now waited patiently to see what Farmer John would do about it.

Farmer John squatted down and took Barney's right ear in his hand.

He looked in that ear, then looked in the left ear.

"Ah ha!" he said, then patted the ground. Barney fell over on his side.

"I'll get you fixed up in nothing flat, Barney Boy. Your left ear is red and swollen inside, but I reckon it'll be just fine once I doctor it."

Barney lay there perfectly still while Farmer John went into the house to get some medicine. When he saw him coming out with a tube in his hand, he started feeling better. Why, even without medicine in his sore ear, he felt better, because now that Farmer John knew his ear was hurting, he was going to fix it. Yep, Barney trusted this man.

When Farmer John looked at April and motioned his head toward Barney, she knew what he meant.

She ran over and knelt down beside her friend and kissed his face.

When she sat down on the ground,
Barney put his head in her lap.

Farmer John squatted down and took the top off the tube of medicine. He squeezed a little into Barney's ear. He worked Barney's ear back and forth and rubbed the side of his face in front of his ear.

"There now, Barney," he said. "That'll make it feel better."

Barney lay there, loving all the attention he was getting. He had his son on one side of him and his friend, April, on the other. What more could he ask for? He closed his eyes.

The throbbing in Barney's ear had almost stopped. But just as he dozed off, the wind picked up, and a breeze blew across his sensitive nose. His long nose quivered and his neck started tingling. The hair on his back and the back of his neck began rising. His eyes flew open, and suddenly, without warning, he sprang to his feet, knocking April backward.

With a low warning growl, Barney whirled and faced the woods, ready for the attacker.

Two

The Rockslide

April knew without having to be told that big trouble was brewing. Her first instinct was to help Barney, but she knew that he could take care of himself. There was someone else there who might need her help more than Barney. She reached down and picked up the puppy, and held it tight.

Just as she started for the back door, a movement in the edge of the woods caught her eye. "Over there, Barney! Look!" she whispered. But her words were wasted on Barney, for the faithful, very protective dog was already moving in that direction.

Farmer John ran for the house. He figured Barney could take care of just about any problem that might arise. But living this far from town, he would feel better with his shotgun or rifle in his hand. With so many varmints roaming the woods, one never knew when one of them might decide to attack one of his cows, or heaven forbid, one of his family.

As dark rumbling storm clouds passed overhead, the family tensed. They didn't know exactly what was about to happen, but they mentally prepared themselves for whatever was coming. Even the twins moved cautiously toward the back door.

A few seconds after he ran into the house, Farmer John came out with his .30-06, cocking it as he ran. The gun might be a little big for whatever was out there, but it would definitely take care of any intruder.

Just then, an animal slunk out of the brush. It had a long body, long legs, and a small head. Its body, without the tail, was about four to four and a half feet long. Its coat was yellowish brown with black spots.

When the big cat saw Barney coming toward it, it stopped in its tracks and crouched low.

Farmer John whispered, "Other than that cougar and jaguar, that's the biggest cat I've ever seen! It looks like a cheetah, but I thought they rounded up all those circus animals that escaped when the circus train wrecked here a while back.

"It looks like a cheetah to me, John. They must have missed that one," Molly answered as she ushered the kids into the house.

"That's it, Molly. Hurry up and get 'em inside! That thing may be tame, and then again, it may not be!"

Farmer John waited to see what Barney was going to do. He didn't want to influence the dog in any way. If he went charging into the woods, Barney would think he wanted him to attack the big cat. And he knew that Barney should not confront the thing.

Barney and the cheetah stared at each other. Neither moved. Barney was smart enough to know that the big cat could kill him if he made a mistake, so he waited and watched. He didn't bat an eye. Not a muscle twitched in the brave coonhound.

The cheetah cried out. Barney growled back, showing his teeth.

"Easy, Boy. Easy," Farmer John whispered. "Don't force it, Barney. Maybe it'll leave on its own."

Barney the Bear Killer didn't seem to hear Farmer John's cautious whisper. He was concentrating on the cheetah. He didn't want the cat to reach the house. He didn't know that his family had gotten safely into the house. All he knew was that he must protect this family. And most of all, he now had a young son to protect. He was not about to let it hurt his son. No way. He'd kill it, if he had to. Yep. He'd kill that big cat dead!

Farmer John had hardly drawn a breath. He was carefully putting one foot in front of the other, easing toward the two. He didn't want to make any sudden moves. He didn't want Barney to attack the cheetah, and he sure didn't want the cheetah to attack Barney. His rifle was at his shoulder, cocked and ready.

Barney was no match for the big cat, but he was not about to let it hurt anyone in his family. He considered his son, and everyone in the house, his family. And since the animals in the woods belonged here, he somehow felt responsible for their safety, too.

"Better back off, Cat!" Barney growled through long snapping teeth.

But the cheetah kept coming, putting one foot in front of the other, inching closer and closer.

Since the cheetah didn't seem to be stopping, Barney made a decision. He sensed that the cheetah was fast, and he knew that if it wasn't going to give up, then he would have to lead it away from the house. He would lead it away from the farm if he had to, and then double back. And if worse came to worse, he would sacrifice his own life, in order to save his family.

Knowing that most cats don't like water, Barney took off, heading for the river.

Looking back over his shoulder, he growled, challenging the big cat to catch him.

The cheetah hesitated only a moment, then raced after Ole Barney. It was running so fast, its body was almost flattened against the ground.

"Go, Barney!" Farmer John yelled, running after the two, with his gun in the air. "Don't let it catch you, Boy! It'll tear you up!"

Watching out the window, the kids were huddled in a little cluster, scared to death. They just knew that the cat was going to kill their daddy and Ole Barney. Molly, on the other

hand, had taken her .22 rifle down
from the rack and was loading it!

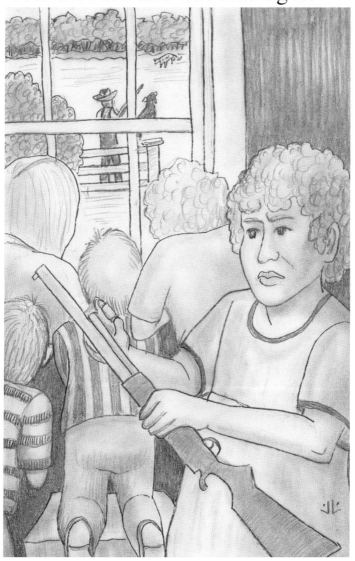

"Is it going to kill Barney?" April asked, with tears in her eyes.

"I doubt it, Honey," Molly said. "I think Barney's trying to lead it away from the house. He's smart. Let's just hope he can outrun it."

The words didn't seem to help April. She was not convinced that everything was going to be okay. Barney was her best friend. And she didn't want to lose him. What would she do without him? This puppy she was squeezing so tightly against her—what would happen to him if Barney died?

"Please come back, Barney!" The words seemed to escape her lips, even though she was trying to be brave for the puppy's sake.

Molly looked at April and saw the tears running down her face. She saw the fear and dread in her blue eyes, and it almost broke her heart. She worried about what her little girl would do if anything happened to the coonhound that she loved so much.

Again, the words tumbled out, "Come back, Barney. Come back!"

"It'll be okay, Sweetie. He'll be fine," Molly said, trying to reassure her.

It was no use. April just knew that it was the end for her best friend. It was the end for Barney.

Three

A Cry for Help

It was amazing how fast those legs could run. That cat was moving on! He was right behind Barney, low to the ground and, with every step, was picking up speed. With only six feet between them, Barney rounded a curve in the trail near the river and made a dive into a big blackberry thicket. He flattened himself on the ground and lay there, perfectly still.

The cheetah went streaking by, certain that Barney was up ahead.

When the big cat passed him, the cunning black-and-tan jumped up and took off, back toward the house. Barney was running faster than he had ever run before. He had to get back to his son. He had to get back to his family. He couldn't leave them alone for long.

When Barney emerged from the woods, Farmer John saw him. He ran for the house, motioning for the dog to follow. They reached the back door at the same time.

April had handed the little pup to Amber to hold, and was anxiously waiting at the window. When she saw her daddy and Barney coming, she ran to the door and threw it open, then stepped aside.

Barney didn't stop and ask for permission to come inside. Not this time. He ran in behind Farmer John. He was happy to see that his son was all right. When Amber put the puppy on the floor, Barney licked the little thing all over its face and neck.

Barney ran to the window and looked in the direction of the river.

"Do you see it, Barney? Is it coming?" Farmer John asked with a worried voice, then turned to Molly. "That thing's big, Molly! Man alive! I hope it doesn't decide to go after the cows. Why, I bet it could eat at least two cows a day!"

On Molly's pretty face was a look that the entire family knew well. It was her *very determined* look. And they all knew what it meant. She was standing there with one hand on her stomach and in her other hand was her gun. There was no way that cat was going to hurt her family. Not if she had anything to say about it. She was carrying another baby in her tummy, and that cheetah was not about to hurt it. She was a protective

mother, and knew how to use a gun!
Why, next to John, she was about the
best shot around. Her daddy had
trained her well.

Farmer John smiled then put his arm around Molly and pulled her close. "It'll be okay, Molly Girl. Maybe that thing won't come back. Maybe it's gone for good."

Looking into his face, she said, "For several years now, my rifle has hung above the fireplace with yours, John."

Farmer John nodded. "You're a fine shot, Molly. I remember when we hunted together a few years ago. No doubt about it, Girl, you're good. But don't do anything to hurt that baby you're carrying."

"I won't. But at the same time, John, I'm not going to let that thing hurt my babies who are already here. I will not stand around and let that happen. If you're gone somewhere and it hurts our kids or our animals,

I'll kill it. If I'm certain that it has hurt one of our kids, I'll kill it dead!"

Farmer John squeezed her hand and said. "I know you would, Molly, and no one could blame you."

Molly walked over to the hearth and placed her rifle back on the rack. When she reached up high, she felt a twinge in her stomach. It was almost as if her unborn baby knew that big cat was near.

She walked into the kitchen and leaned against the counter. When she turned and looked at the boys, their eyes were big. They looked scared. Molly suddenly realized that they had never seen her with a gun. Seeing her holding a gun in her hands must have scared them to death! Why, it's no wonder the poor little things were frightened.

Farmer John saw the look on the boys' faces. He sat down in his chair and slapped his legs. "Get over here, you little scalawags. I haven't had my hugs today."

The boys ran over and crawled onto their daddy's knees. Each one gave him a great big hug.

Farmer John said, "Now, that's more like it. That makes me feel much better."

The twins grinned. Lately, they had started grinning just like their daddy.

"Can that thing get in the house, Daddy? Can it tear down the door or jump through a window? Is it going to tear us up and eat us?" Jack asked.

"Nosiree! Not if your mama and I have anything to say about it. Do you boys honestly think that we're gonna let something that bad happen to you? I'll tell you what, if I'm outside, your mama will be in the house with you. And if she's outside, you'll be right under her two wings, and she'll take good care of you. Seeing her with that gun was a real surprise, huh, Boys?"

The twins nodded their heads. Then, using his index finger on his right hand, Jake curled his finger up and motioned for his daddy to lean down.

When Farmer John leaned his head down and turned his ear toward Jake's mouth, Jake whispered, "Mama had a gun, Daddy. Why did she have a gun?"

"Can Mama shoot that big gun, Daddy? If she shoots it, will she get in trouble?" John asked.

"Nah, she's old enough to shoot a gun, Boys. She's a good shot, too," Farmer John whispered. The boys seemed relieved.

The next afternoon, Barney and Farmer John headed down the lane to bring the milk cows in. It was time to start the evening milking.

The entire time they were rounding up the cows and heading them for the dairy barn, Barney was alert. He had a wary eye out for the cheetah. When he wasn't nipping at a stubborn cow's hoof to get her moving, he was scanning the edge of the woods and the trees by the pond as he trotted through the pasture.

Farmer John was on guard, too. The thing he was afraid of was that the cheetah would begin killing and eating his farm animals. That was a scary thought. The animals that lived on his place were not just animals. They provided his family with what they needed to survive on this farm. For instance, the chickens provided eggs and fried chicken every Sunday. The plump older hens were stewed for delicious chicken and dumplings.

Also, the family liked baked chicken. Every member of the family loved chicken, no matter how it was fixed. A couple of pigs each year provided pork. A steer provided tender beef. You get the picture, don't you?

They were almost to the barn when Barney's skin began crawling. He stopped dead still. Only his head moved as he quickly looked from side to side. He whirled around and looked behind them. He didn't see a thing, but something was out there. And then, the wind shifted just a bit, and he got a whiff of the cheetah.

Barney growled his infamous growl. It was a low warning growl. It was a growl all the animals knew. Everyone on the farm knew his growl and they knew that it meant, "Get off this farm! Back off! Leave now!"

Barney the Bear Killer crouched low, waiting.

And that's when the cheetah emerged from the trees.

Well, evidently, it didn't know Barney's low warning growl and what it meant. Or else it was brave. It had to be brave, because it just stood, growling at Barney. It ran toward Barney and then ran back the other way. It seemed to be daring Barney to chase it, or maybe to catch it, if he could. Or perhaps it was challenging Barney to a fight. Or could it be that the cheetah had already made his home on the farm somewhere and was trying to assert its presence? Maybe it was saying, "Come on, Dog! You wanna fight? Either you accept me and let me stay, or I'll kill you right now!"

Well now, that was a challenge that Ole Barney could not turn down.

He looked at Farmer John. After the first encounter with the cat, he knew he'd better check with his master, first.

Farmer John said, "Just cool it, Barney. Let that big cat stew awhile. Don't do anything rash. Let's let it make the first move. Let's wait and see what its next move is. Just don't let it get too close to the cows. Watch it, Barney."

Well, sometimes we mind what we're told, and sometimes we don't. Barney was no exception. At times, he acted just like a little kid. He was standing there, ready and hopefully able, to defend Farmer John's Place.

Suddenly the cheetah growled, whirled and ran for the woods! It glanced back a couple of times to see if the dog had accepted its challenge.

Ole Barney completely ignored Farmer John's words. He took off in a heart-pounding, high-speed chase. And even when Farmer John yelled, "No, Barney! You come back here!" the black-and-tan keeping going.

Farmer John now stood, shaking his head. "That dadblamed dog is so fired up, he won't listen. I can't let him tackle that thing all by himself. It's too big. It'll kill him for sure. I'd better leave the milking and help him get rid of that varmint. He'll either have to run it off the farm or kill it, 'cause that cheetah thinks it's here to stay."

Wiping his brow as he headed in the direction Ole Barney had taken, Farmer John again shook his head. His gun was loaded, and there were shells in the pocket of his overalls. "It's too bad he didn't mind," he said. "Ole Barney's been a real good dog. I'd sure hate to lose him."

Barney chased the cheetah to a cave near the base of a hill on the far side of Farmer John's Place.

In the distance, a thunderstorm was brewing. It was coming up fast. Barney had noticed a little lightning in the west, but he figured the storm wouldn't get to the farm until after the evening milking was over and they were safely in the house. He couldn't quit now. He was relentless in his pursuit of the cat. He wanted it to leave the farm. He wanted it gone!

Barney looked at the cave. He remembered it. That's where Brutus lived. Maybe Brutus had moved out. Or maybe the cheetah had made its home in one of the other tunnels in the cave. It did have several tunnels.

Barney heard the wind picking up. Suddenly, thunder boomed and a bolt of lightning streaked downward. It struck a tree beside him. He fell to the ground, addled. Another jag of lightning hit a boulder on top of the hill. The boulder began tumbling, slow at first, but it picked up speed. It rolled down the hill, bringing with it all the smaller rocks in its path.

Barney looked up. He wasn't sure what to do. While he was trying to decide which way to run, the rockslide swept him up. He tumbled down the hill, right into the river.

Farmer John both heard and saw the rockslide. But he didn't see his dog being swept into the raging river. He stopped at the base of the hill and called out, "Barney! Where are you? If you can you hear me, answer me!"

If Barney could have heard the call, he would have heard both hurt and something very close to panic in Farmer John's voice. But he couldn't hear his master. He was down deep in the choppy water.

The storm had reached the farm and was lashing at Farmer John's place. It was affecting everything and everyone in its path. Thunder was booming, bouncing back and forth between the trees. Jagged bolts of lightning were hitting the ground. The storm was an electrical storm! And it was bad!

"Barney!" Farmer John called again and again, digging frantically at the rock slide with his two hands. He stood up and took off his hat. "If Ole Barney's under these rocks and he's conscious, he'll answer me."

After searching for a long time, Farmer John sat down on a medium-sized boulder and slowly bowed his head. "I reckon that old saying, *a dog is man's best friend,* is true." Then, with his elbows on his knees and his head in his hands, he wept.

Ole Barney had surfaced again, but because of the raging storm, did not hear Farmer John's call.

Suddenly, a dead log, persuaded by the strong wind, rolled right off the high bank and hit the swift water. It came cruising down the river and bumped into Barney.

Even with the heavy rain that was falling, and the tossing in the water, the coonhound detected a light scent of *raccoon* on the old dead log.

Before the water could carry the log away from Barney, he climbed on it and inched from one end to the other, sniffing.

Now, in the predicament he was in, Barney didn't need to be thinking about catching a raccoon but, true to the nature of a coonhound, he just couldn't help it.

Soon, the swift water carried the log into the middle of the river.

Barney suddenly realized that he had two options. He could jump into the water and try swimming to the bank. Or he could stay with the log and wait for the river to make a turn so that hopefully the log would bump into the bank. After getting a knot on his head, he couldn't seem to remember all the turns in the river, even though he knew the river well.

Barney now made a decision. He jumped into the water and began swimming. He slowly pulled himself toward the bank. But the driving wind and rain kept pushing him back to the middle of the river.

Through the rain he saw the bank. He tried desperately to reach it, but the going was slow. Finally, an exhausted black-and-tan coonhound dragged himself out on the bank.

Four

Where's June Bug?

Molly hurried out the back door with a clothes basket in her arms. Her clean clothes were dry. So when she heard the storm coming, she ran to get them in before they got wet again. She ran across the yard to the clothesline. She took the clothes off the line and put them in the basket. When it was full, she turned to go back into the house, but stopped. She suddenly felt so strange. Something was wrong. She looked all around. Her skin began tingling and crawling when she suddenly realized that one of her children seemed to be missing. There were only four children in sight! She saw Amber and the twins. April was sitting quietly on the back porch with her eyes on the woods. But where was Ashley?

Earlier, Ashley, or *June Bug*, as her daddy called her, had been in the backyard, playing with a basketball. She had been tossing it at a tree, and when it had bounced off the tree, she tried to catch it. The last time she tossed the ball, it had hit the tree and bounced back toward her. And even though she jumped as high as she could, it had bounced over her head and rolled out across the yard. When she had bent over to pick it up, she had accidentally kicked it. The kick had sent the basketball rolling. She had tried to catch it, but it had rolled behind an azalea bush that grew along the side of the house. When she ran behind the bush to get it, she had tripped over something that was crouching there. She had fallen and hit her head against the house.

Ashley had sat up and tried to get to her feet, but something had hit her in the side. It had knocked her down. Before she could recover, strong jaws had grasped one of her arms and had dragged her toward the dense woods. When she had opened her mouth to scream, not a sound had come out. Then, perhaps she had passed out because of the lick on her head. Or maybe she had gotten a look at the animal that was dragging her and had fainted because she was so scared.

"Have you kids seen Ashley?" Molly called.

Amber shrugged her shoulders, and the twin boys shook their heads.

April looked up. "I saw her. She was playing with her basketball. It bounced off that big tree and rolled out across the yard. It kept rolling. The last time I saw her, Mama, she was running after it."

Molly glanced in the direction April was pointing. Then, carrying the basket full of clothes, she looked at April and nodded at the back door.

April jumped up and held the door open for her mama.

Molly carried the basket into her bedroom and set it on the foot of the bed. She went down the hall and through the house, calling Ashley's name.

When Ashley didn't answer, Molly ran to the front room and took her .22 down off the rack on the wall. She made sure it was loaded and then went straight to the cabinet where Farmer John kept his shells. She grabbed a handful of .22 shells and put them in her apron pocket. When she reached the back door, she stood for a minute with her hand on the screen door. She thought about the new baby she was carrying in her tummy. She knew she would have to be careful. But, at the same time, June Bug was missing.

Molly had good instincts, and she was a very good mother. She realized that, with Farmer John gone right now, it might very well be up to her to save their youngest daughter. She took a deep breath, opened the screen door, and walked out onto the porch just as it began drizzling.

When the boys saw their mama with the gun in her hand, their eyes got big. They stood perfectly still, and stared at her.

Gently pushing the boys toward the back porch, Amber realized what her mama was thinking. "I'll go with you, Mama. I'll help you find her. April can stay here with the boys."

"No, Amber. You are the oldest. You stay here. I'll go to the barn and then the chicken house and look for her. If I can't find her, I'll come back and ring the bell. That will tell your daddy that we have a problem here. He'll come running. And if, for some reason he doesn't, I'll walk along the edge of the woods and call out her name, over and over. If she's within the sound of my voice, she'll answer. She'll answer...if she can."

"What if she doesn't, Mama?" Amber asked, with fear in her voice. "You're not going into the woods after her, are you? That cheetah is out there!"

"I will if I have to, Honey. But only if I have to," Molly answered.

All the color left Amber's face. She grew pale and began pleading, "Please don't, Mama. Please don't go into the woods. If that cheetah is in the woods, he'll kill you, Mama! He'll kill you! You know that!"

Molly hesitated a second then turned and looked at her daughter.

"I may have to, Honey. At the moment, I'm not sure what I'll do. I'll have to make that decision when the time comes."

"All right, Mama. Do what you have to do, but please be careful," Amber said. "I don't know what I'd do if anything happened to you. I don't know what any of us would do without you, Mama. We love you."

Just then, Molly felt a twinge in her tummy. Perhaps it was a tiny foot kicking her to remind her that she needed to take it easy. Whatever it was, a foot or a stretched-out fist, it made Molly stop and think. After all, she was responsible, not only for her own safety, but for the safety of her unborn child.

That did it. Molly dropped her head. Then she looked up toward the stormy heavens and closed her eyes.

With one hand on her stomach, Molly looked down at Amber and whispered, "You're right, Honey.

I'm going to check the shed, the hay barn, and the chicken house. I'll walk along the edge of the trees, but I won't go into the woods. Now, get the kids inside and keep them there."

Amber's eyes were brimming with tears. She said, "Okay, Mama. We'll keep the puppy inside, too."

Molly kissed her oldest child on the cheek, and gave her a big hug. She put on a brave smile, lifted her chin a bit, and with a determined walk, headed for the barn. It was one of the special places where the kids loved to play. She knew that they felt safe when they played in the hay barn with the big double doors shut.

If the cheetah had taken Ashley, it would be a horrible thing if she found them and her gun was empty. She could imagine standing there, carefully taking aim, and then getting nothing but an empty *click* when she pulled the trigger. So, once again, she stopped and checked her gun. Her single-shot .22 rifle was **loaded!**

Molly checked the hay barn and then looked up at the loft. She called, "Ashley! Are you playing in the hay loft?"

There was no answer, so she left the barn and went to the side shed where Barney and his little son slept. Same thing. No Ashley. She hurried to the chicken house and checked it. Again, no Ashley. Then she heard a sound. She wasn't sure what it was. It was a weird sound, let's say, something between a snarl and a growl.

She whirled around, then ran to the back of the hay barn, thinking maybe the sound had come from back there. There was nothing there except Marty. He was standing there, grazing. He hadn't made that sound. She heard it again. With her heart racing, she screamed, "Ashley!"

She ran around the barn and stopped. The children were standing with their faces pressed against the windows, watching her through the rain. She put one hand on her tummy and patted it. "Stay calm, Molly," she said. "Stay calm for the sake of this little one. Don't hurt it."

Gripping her rifle in one hand, she walked slowly toward the woods. When she neared the trees, she stopped and called Ashley's name.

There was no answer, so she walked along, parallel with the trees, as far as she dared. The entire time, she was calling her little girl's name.

There was a sudden movement off to the side. She just knew it was her little girl. Her heart began racing. "Is that you, Ashley?" she called. "Answer me!"

In the blink of an eye, a spotted, yellowish brown streak came out of the dense woods and sprang at her. It landed on her shoulder and they both hit the ground.

Pure instinct made Molly throw one arm up to cover her face. Then she tried to raise the rifle that was in her other hand. She couldn't raise her arm. The thing was on top of her, pinning her down.

"Get off me!" she screamed.

Someone up there was watching over Molly that day, because the big cat backed off. It stood, three or four feet from Molly, looking at her.

Molly slowly got to her feet and bravely faced the cheetah. A thought went racing through her mind. This cheetah might be one of the animals that had escaped when the circus train had wrecked that night after the circus performance, or it might have escaped from a nearby zoo. If it was from the circus, it might be halfway tame. It hadn't acted mean when it was performing at the circus that night. But if it had escaped from a zoo, it would revert to its wild side. Either way, she knew that if she ran from the cheetah, it would chase her. She decided to bluff her way through this very difficult situation. She raised the rifle and put it against her shoulder. "If you attack me again, I'll kill you! I mean it!" she said.

The sight of a gun must have been new to the cheetah, because it backed up a step and looked at her, narrowing its eyes.

With a pounding heart and eyes shinning, her finger began squeezing the trigger. "Where's my little girl? Where is she? Have you killed her? Did you take her into the woods and kill and eat her? Did you?"

Molly stood with her finger on the trigger. What should she do? Should she go ahead and kill him? When the cat didn't move, she took another step toward it. "So help me, if you've killed Ashley, I'll kill you!" she screamed.

The unexpected pains that shot through her stomach were crippling. She fell to her knees, but she held on to the gun.

The cheetah stood for a second and then whirled and ran for the woods.

Five

Survival

"Barney! Can you hear me? Answer me, Boy!" Farmer John called again and again. Finally, he heard a whine. It sounded like it was coming from the river, so he ran to the river and looked out in the water. He saw nothing in the water. He ran down the bank. Suddenly, he tripped over something. When he stopped and looked down, his heart skipped a beat. With a lump in his throat and a pounding heart, he quickly dropped to his knees.

"Barney!" he cried. He picked up the dog and held him close.

On their way to the farmhouse, Farmer John carried Ole Barney. He glanced down every few steps to see how his usually faithful, but recently disobedient dog was doing.

"You're gonna be just fine, Boy. When I get you to the house and get you all dried off and warmed up a mite, you'll feel better. Yessiree. You're gonna be just fine.

It wasn't long before Barney wanted down. He wasn't helpless. He could walk by himself. He didn't want Farmer John to think that he had to be babied. Even a rock slide, a knot on his head and near drowning couldn't slow him down. Not much. He was supposed to guard this farm. But what about that big cheetah cat? He knew he hadn't minded his boss. But when you stop and think about it, how in the world was he expected to stand still and let that thing mess with anyone or anything on Farmer John's place? He might have caught it, too, if it hadn't been for that rock slide. He would have really whipped-up on that cheetah. Yep! That's what he would have done if he had caught it. Man alive! That big cat would have left this farm so fast that there would have been nothing left behind it but a trail of smoke!

Understanding now that Barney wanted to walk home on his own, Farmer John put him down. He did watch him for a little while to make sure he was okay, knowing that a bad limp might indicate a pulled muscle in his leg, or it could mean he had a broken bone. Either one was serious. He didn't want Ole Barney to suffer.

They were almost home when
Barney stopped in his tracks.

Glancing back, Farmer John
asked, "What's wrong, Barney Boy?
Is one of your legs hurting you?"
That's when he noticed the bristling
hair on Barney's neck and back.

Farmer John's muscles tensed. He knew without having to be told that the cheetah was near. He figured that as tired as Ole Barney was right now, the cheetah was about the only thing that could rile him.

"Come on. Let's get on home, Boy. No sense in taking on that big cat tonight," Farmer John said as he bent down to pat Barney's side.

Barney didn't want to, but he knew it would be best if he followed his friend. The part about not taking on that cat tonight hit home.

It had almost stopped raining by the time they reached the back door. Just as Farmer John touched the door knob, the door flew open and four kids sailed out, right smack into his arms. Then he saw the looks on their faces. Were the looks worried looks?

Maybe they were. Or maybe the looks on those four faces were scared looks.

"What's wrong with you kids? Where's June Bug and your mama?

"We don't know where they are, Daddy! When Ashley disappeared, Mama went to look for her. But it's been a long time since she left. She hasn't come back and neither has Ashley. Will you go look for them, Daddy? Will you?" they asked.

A sick feeling flooded through Farmer John when he remembered the way Barney had tensed up or *alerted* at a certain place on the trail when they were on their way home. He looked down at Barney and gave him a pat, then motioned for him to go in the house. He was not a house dog, but he needed some quiet rest.

"Keep Barney in the house for awhile. He's tired right now. He just survived a race with a cheetah, a rock slide, and a raging river."

That was when a shot rang out! When they heard the crack of a rifle, a couple of the kids screamed, and the other two hurried for the door. Farmer John recognized the sound. It was Molly's .22 rifle.

With a grim look on his face, he said, "Get in the house, all of you! Get in there and lock both doors. Don't come out and don't let the pup out! I'm going to look for June Bug and your mama. Nicki, look at the clock, and if I'm not back here in thirty minutes, let Barney out." He went down the steps two at a time.

Amber nodded. "Okay, Daddy. Are you going to find Ashley and

Mama and bring them back with you? Are you, Daddy?"

"I'll do my best, Nicki!" he said. *Nicki* was a nickname he had given Amber when she was a baby.

"Yessiree!" he uttered, then clenched his teeth. "I'm gonna do my dead-level best. If that cat hurts June Bug or Molly, I'll kill it dead! I'll kill it deader than a doornail!"

Farmer John was running now, with his .30-06 clutched in his hand. He was heading back to the place on the trail where Barney had *alerted.*

When he rounded a sharp curve in the trail, he suddenly veered right. He had almost run over Molly and June Bug. Molly's face was grim. She was clutching her .22 with one hand and her tummy with the other. Ashley had a grip on Molly's dress.

"Molly! You found June Bug!" Farmer John said as he dropped down beside them. Then he noticed that they were sitting back to back.

It took only seconds to size-up the situation. They must be sitting that way so that they could see any approaching animal. That was it! They were under attack!

Farmer John took Molly's hand in his to help her to her feet. When his fingers touched her wrist, he quickly jerked his hand back and his eyebrows shot up.

"Good grief, Molly Girl! Your pulse is pounding! Are you scared or in labor? You're not gonna have that baby right here on the trail, are you? No! You can't do that! Nosiree! You can't have that little tyke out here in the woods. We're not gonna let you, are we June Bug?"

The little girl, still clutching her mama's dress, shook her head and answered, "No, Daddy."

Farmer John was getting a whiff of a familiar scent. He took Molly's .22 rifle, held it up to his nose and sniffed. Yep, it had been fired!

"Did you kill that thing, Molly? Did you kill the cheetah?" he asked.

Molly didn't say yes and she didn't say no. She said, "That thing had Ashley, John, but I found her and I got her away from it!"

"Who, Molly? Who had her? The cheetah? Did that dadblasted cheetah hurt her?"

"I found her, John. I found her," Molly kept saying as she rocked back and forth, obviously in pain. "I was trying to get her home, but something attacked us. I shot it, John."

"You shot the circus cheetah? Did you really? Did you kill it, Molly?" he asked.

"Not the cheetah. It was bigger! It came from out of nowhere. It must have dropped from a tree limb, John. It landed on my shoulders. I tried to keep Ashley behind me, but she kept getting out in front of me. She was trying to protect me the entire time I was trying to protect her. I couldn't get a clear shot. But it kept coming closer and closer, and when it lunged at us again, I had no choice. I aimed as straight as I could, and pulled the trigger. I hit it, John. I know I hit it."

"It's a wonder it didn't tear you to pieces, Molly. Wounding a wild animal and not finishing it off is very risky. I reckon it's about the most dangerous thing that can happen to anyone. In a way, you're lucky, Girl. You're both lucky! If that cheetah had joined in, you know what would have happened, don't you? Both of you would have been goners. Yep! That's what would've happened!"

"I know that a wounded animal is dangerous. But I had no choice, John. I didn't want it to kill us. I was trying to save Ashley and the baby, and myself."

Molly's face suddenly changed. The pains in her stomach seemed to have eased off. She stopped rocking back and forth. She looked up at her husband and asked, "Do you want to know the strangest part of all, John? The cheetah actually got between us, like he was trying to protect us."

"Or maybe he wanted to save you for himself," Farmer John said, under his breath.

"I'm serious, John. I'm serious. Earlier, the cheetah had attacked me.

But when I yelled at it, it backed off. Perhaps the years it has been with the circus has taught it to respect others. It was going into the woods, but when I screamed, it turned back. When it came running toward us, I thought it was going to attack us, so I threw up my gun. But before I could squeeze the trigger, that other thing dropped from a limb above us and landed on me. It almost scared me to death, John! It scared Ashley, too."

Farmer John was on one side of Molly and Ashley was on the other. They were slowly moving down the trail toward home.

Trying to keep Molly's mind off the obvious pain she was having, Farmer John kept talking. "And then what happened, Molly Girl? Did the cheetah attack you, too?"

"That's what I'm trying to tell you, John. I finally realized that the cheetah might be trying to save us from the animal that had dropped on me. The cheetah fought with that thing for a long time, and when it backed off, the cheetah chased it into the woods. We haven't seen it since. We haven't seen the cheetah either. It was scary, John! It was really scary!"

Ashley had finally recovered her voice. She said, "It was, Daddy. It was so scary. I could just imagine it eating Mama and me. And I could just see it running off toward our house, licking its lips in anticipation. I bet those boys and Amber and April would fill it up, for sure!"

Farmer John smiled. June Bug had a good imagination, all right. But this time, she didn't have to use her imagination. She had just had a close encounter with the real thing.

Molly said, "Look for it, John. And if you find it, finish killing it. I don't like that thing, but I don't want it to suffer either."

"Okay, Molly. I'll take a look, but I need to hurry and get you home. I think maybe you're gonna have that baby a few weeks early," he said.

He started back along the trail, then stopped and ran back to Molly. "What was it, Molly? What did you shoot at?" he asked. "You haven't said. You keep calling it 'that thing'. I need to know what to watch for."

Molly shook her head. "I know what it looked like, John, but we haven't seen one of them around here in a long time."

"Well, Molly, are you gonna tell

me or do you want me to guess?"

"Someday I'll tell you what I think it was, John. If I told you now, you would just laugh."

"I won't laugh. Now, come on, what was it? Spit it out, Girl!"

"No, John. Not today."

Farmer John grinned and then headed back down the trail to look for the wounded animal. He hadn't gone ten feet when his eyes picked up spots of blood. The spots turned into a steady dribble, or thin line. The trail wasn't hard to follow now.

"Well, Molly hit it all right. Thing is, I'm not sure what she hit. And she may not know, for sure," he thought.

After about twenty more feet, the blood dwindled down to spots, and finally stopped, altogether.

"Hmm," Farmer John said. "Now, this tells me that 'the thing' stopped bleeding, right about here. This means it's probably okay now, and he's out there somewhere, alive and kicking."

A horrible thought suddenly thought ran through Farmer John's mind. He knew that wild animals, like some criminals, will double back and return to the scene of the crime. This thing may have done just that. He might have circled and gone back to finish what he had started with Molly and June Bug.

Farmer John's heart stood still. Then he took off down the trail in a dead run, back to the place where he had left June Bug and Molly.

Just before he reached them, he heard June Bug scream, "Mama!"

Then he heard what sounded like a groan.

The first thing he saw when he got close to where he had left them, was Barney coming down the trail.

The black-and-tan coonhound was moving fast, with his nose to the ground. He was definitely tracking something. When he looked up and saw Molly and Ashley, he picked up speed. Then he saw Farmer John coming from the other direction.

Farmer John was not the only one who had heard Ashley's scream. Barney had heard it, too. And when Barney saw Molly's face, he knew that something was wrong.

Even if he has not seen her face, he immediately sensed that she was in trouble. Ole Barney had a sixth sense about some things.

Barney bristled. His head tilted back and his nose began wiggling. He knew that the cheetah was near. When Ashley had screamed, he just knew that she had spotted the big cat.

When Barney saw Molly on her knees, he ran up beside her and braced himself, so that she could lean on him if she wanted to.

Molly leaned on Barney until Farmer John reached her.

Farmer John picked her up in his arms and whispered, "It's okay, Molly Girl. I'm gonna get you home. You and that little one are gonna be just fine. Let's go, June Bug. Stay right in front of me. Okay? I don't want you out of my sight."

"Okay, Daddy. Is Mama going to be all right?" she asked with a worried look on her face.

"Your mama is one tough lady, June Bug. Whatever is ahead, she can handle it," he said with a smile. "I'd bet my life on that."

Farmer John looked at Barney and said, "You watch our backside, Barney. Don't let anything slip up on us, Boy. You know what to do if something tries that."

Barney the Bear Killer's face showed that he understood what his master was saying.

With hope in his heart and Molly and their unborn baby in his arms, Farmer John headed for home at a steady but very careful walk.

Ashley was trying to be brave. She was fighting back the tears. She looked back several times to check on Barney. At times she almost fell behind her daddy's long strides.

Six

Return of the Cheetah

Thoughts were racing through Farmer John's mind. "Should I start boiling some water, and send for the doctor? Or should I try to get Molly to town?" he muttered. "That's risky. A fast bumpy ride in the truck might cause her to lose the baby."

Farmer John was so consumed with Molly's safety and the safety of the unborn baby that those thoughts completely filled his head.

When he saw the house, it was all he could do to keep from running.

The kids were all watching through the windows. They opened the door before he had to kick it with his foot to let them know that he was home.

Farmer John turned around and looked for Barney. The dog was on the back porch looking back along the trail that led to the woods. He wanted to make absolutely sure the cheetah hadn't followed them home.

Farmer John took Molly to the bedroom and laid her on the bed.

The five children followed their daddy and mama into the bedroom. No one said a word. They stood just inside the door quietly watching.

Farmer John took Molly's shoes off and put a light quilt over her. He turned around and waved his hand toward the hallway. The kids tiptoed out of the room.

When they reached the living room, Farmer John looked at his five kids and said, "Your mama's in labor. You girls know what that means."

The girls said, "We know what it means, Daddy."

Farmer John looked at the twins and said, "You boys know that your mama is gonna have another baby. Well, it's time for the baby to be born. Now I want you kids to do exactly as I say. No arguments. Amber, I want you to hurry over to Joe Clark's house. Tell him that I need him to go get Doc Miller. Ask his wife if she can come back here with you so that she can help your mama. Now, tell Joe to hurry!"

"How do I get there, Daddy?" Amber asked. "Are you taking me or do I walk?"

Farmer John did not hesitate. He pulled his truck keys out of his pocket and held them out to Amber. "You think you can drive the truck, Nicki? If you do, take these keys. And hurry, Girl! Time's a wastin'!"

Amber grabbed the keys out of her daddy's hand and flew out the back door. She hoped she could keep the pickup truck in the road. At least, between the ditches.

Farmer John turned his attention to April. "I want you to boil some water, J. J.! Put several pans of water on the stove and get them hot as fast as you can!" he ordered.

When April hesitated, he said, "Go, Girl! Move it!"

April whirled and hurried to the kitchen. They heard pots and pans rattling as she filled them with water.

"What can we do, Daddy?" the boys asked.

Farmer John looked down. The twins had very worried looks on their faces.

"Well, Boys," he said. "We're gonna need some nice clean white rags."

He looked at Ashley and asked, "You okay now, June Bug? Do you think you can take the boys to the linen closet and get two or three of our older white sheets and bring them to the kitchen?"

"I'm feeling fine now, Daddy. The boys and I will get the sheets."

"Hurry, June Bug! That baby's just itching to get out of your mama's tummy and say, 'Hi y'all'!"

That brought giggles from Jack and Jake. Ashley just grinned.

Farmer John went quietly down the hall and peeked in their bedroom. Molly was asleep. He held out his hands and looked at them. As usual, they could stand a little soap and water. He hurried to the kitchen sink and rolled up his sleeves. April had the water to the boiling stage, so he took one of the pots of hot water from the stove and poured a good amount into a bowl. He dipped his fingers in the steaming hot water four or five times and then scrubbed them with lye soap. He rinsed the soap off them, and then looked at April.

He said, "We're gonna need lots of hot water, Girl. You're doing good. Keep it coming."

Suddenly, a big grin came over Farmer John's face. "What do you think we should name the little tyke,

J. J.? Have you or the others thought of a name?" he asked.

"I've been trying to think of a name for the baby, Daddy. But so far, I haven't thought of a good one." She hesitated a moment and said, "Maybe Mama has already picked a name, Daddy. Have you asked her?"

Farmer John shook his head. "Reckon I thought we had plenty of time. Well, I'd better get in there with your mama."

Farmer John hurried to their bedroom. Molly was still asleep. Her face was pale and drawn.

Farmer John knelt down on one knee. He put his ear toward Molly's face. Her breathing was steady. "Good," was the one word his lips formed. He bowed his head and closed his eyes for several seconds.

Then he sat down in a chair that was near Molly's side of the bed. He rubbed the chair arms with his hands. Molly loved this chair. She always sat in it every morning when she was putting on her shoes. It had been his mama's chair. It was Molly's now. When he thought about his mama, he always smiled. He wished she could be here now to see this new baby being born. She would know what to do and exactly how to help Molly. He wished with all his heart that she hadn't died when he was little. He had loved his mama when she was alive, and he still missed her. After all these years, he still missed her. She would have loved his children.

The sound of a truck stopping in front of the house brought him back to the present. He knew by the sound of the engine that it was his truck. Good for Nicki. She had not wrecked the truck. She had made it safely to Joe's house and was back with Joe's wife.

He ran out the front door and greeted them. As Mrs. Clark hurried to Molly, he gave Amber a hug and said, "You did real good, Nicki. I'm proud of you. I don't see any dents in the fenders."

Amber was obviously relieved to be safely home. "How's Mama, Daddy? Is she okay? Has she had the baby yet? Is the baby okay? Is it a boy or a girl?"

"Hey, slow down, Young Lady! I'm used to you talking fast, but you're going a little too fast for me," he chuckled. "Now, let's see if I can answer your questions in the order

you asked them. She's okay. No.
Yes. I hope so. And, I don't know."

That's when Jack sailed out the front door, followed by Jake. Then Barney's warning growl could be heard. "Hurry, Daddy!" Jake yelled. "The cheetah's in the back yard!"

Farmer John pulled the twins to him. With an arm around each one, he said quietly, "Be quiet, Boys. You'll wake up your mama. Don't worry yourselves about that cheetah. I'll take care of it."

Farmer John ushered everyone into the house, then hurried to the phone. He called the sheriff's office in town and informed them that the cheetah had turned up again.

"The sheriff will notify the right people, and they'll be out tomorrow to capture the cheetah. In the meantime," Farmer John said, "don't go outside. That applies to all of you."

He looked at Barney. "That big cat's back, Barney. But you already know that, don't you? Stay alert. And don't do anything until I say it's okay. Understand?"

Barney the Bear Killer looked into Farmer John's eyes. There was no doubt about his expression. The black-and-tan coonhound understood. And this time, he would obey his master.

They went to the window and looked out. At first, they couldn't see anything that resembled a cheetah. Then a low warning growl started deep in Barney's chest and finally escaped his throat.

"Barney sees it," Farmer John whispered.

They looked in the direction the dog was looking and spotted a long yellowish brown tail with black spots curled around the front side of the oak tree in the backyard.

"There it is. See? Don't anyone scream out," Farmer John cautioned. "I don't want your mama upset."

The kids nodded their heads. But Barney was faunching at the bit! The hair on the coonhound's back and the back of his neck was standing straight up! Anyone looking at him could tell that he was just dying to get a throat hold on that cheetah.

"Easy, Boy. Just take it easy." Farmer John's soothing words were not one bit comforting to Barney. He was upset with this dadblasted cat! To think that it would have the nerve to come into this yard like it was something special! Barney had one foot on the window sill, and he was snapping his razor-sharp teeth. And a tiny bit of saliva was dripping from his mouth.

"John!" Molly's scream split the dead quiet wide open! Well, it wasn't really a scream. It meant, "Please come here this instant, John! I need you! We need you! Hurry!"

Farmer John looked at the kids. Then, after a glance at Ole Barney, he hurried to the bedroom where things were beginning to happen.

Just as he rushed through the door he heard a *"Push!"* and then a *"Whaaaaa."* And then nothing. All was quiet in the master bedroom.

Farmer John's eyes focused on Molly's shining face. Her face was wet. But she was lying there smiling. She was happy. She had heard the baby cry and knew it was okay.

Mrs. Clark gently placed a pink blanket, with something soft and warm inside it, in Molly's arms.

Farmer John had a big grin as he looked at the two. What a picture!

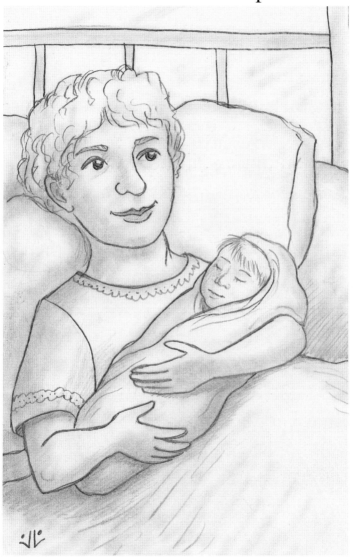

He leaned down and kissed his wife on the forehead. He was proud of her for being so brave. With the other five children she'd had a doctor present. But due to the unforeseen circumstances, there simply wasn't time to get to the doctor.

About that time, Doc Miller and Joe showed up. Joe stopped at the door and looked in, but Doc Miller hurried on into the room.

"Looks like you took care of things just fine, Mrs. Clark. And I'm glad. I'd hate to see anything happen to this young woman. These children are going to need her. Especially this little lady."

Doc Miller leaned over and took the baby from Molly's arms. He held her up close to his face and looked her over real good. Then he gently placed her on the side of the bed and unwrapped her just like he would unwrap a fragile Christmas present.

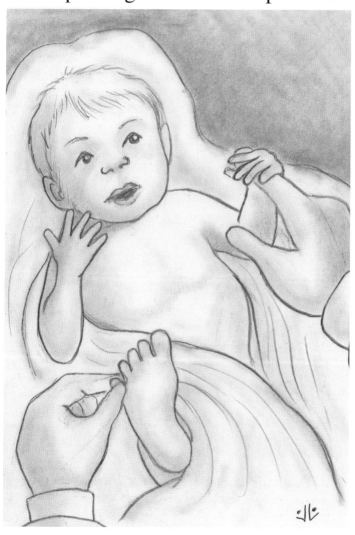

The doctor examined the baby girl with a fine-tooth comb. He pulled on each arm and each wrist and each finger. He pulled on each leg. He carefully twisted each foot, one at a time. He wiggled each toe. He listened to her heart. He looked into each ear. He checked each eye and then looked into her little mouth.

Doc Miller smiled and nodded. "This little lady has a strong tongue. I'm glad, because I know for a fact that girls like to talk."

Molly blushed and reached for the baby.

Farmer John threw his head back and laughed. "That's real good, Doc. And that's very very true." This time, he bent down and gave the baby a big kiss on one of her rosy cheeks.

Molly nodded toward the door. "You men may leave this room now." She looked down at the baby and whispered, "We need our beauty rest, don't we, Faith?"

At the mention of the name, the men stopped and looked back.

"That was your grandmother's name, Molly. It's a beautiful name. When did you decide to name her Faith?" Farmer John asked with a surprised look on his face.

"When I though I might lose this little baby out there in the woods, John, I started praying. And with all my heart I believe it was faith that brought me safely through this entire episode. Faith, you, and Barney. You don't mind me naming her Faith, do you, John? I want you to like the name, too."

"I love the name, Molly." They heard panting at the door and turned. There stood Barney, grinning.

Farmer John slapped his leg and Barney crossed the room. He studied the baby wrapped in the pink blanket with a great deal of interest.

That's when they heard a couple of gasps and some giggles and even a squeal. The kids couldn't wait. They had invited themselves into their mama and daddy's bedroom. They just had to see the new baby.

The five kids walked up to the bed, one at a time. They didn't try to hold it. They just looked it over real good.

This time, Farmer John didn't let *beauty go first*. This time he let the boys be first in line. Perhaps he figured that since they were younger, and had been considered the *babies of the family* for some time now, they might have some adjusting to do. Well, it worked. They accepted little Faith right then and there.

The three girls were tickled pink that it was another girl. This was most definitely a point in their favor. Now the girls would outnumber the boys for sure.

Well, Farmer John was walking in high cotton that day! All day long.

When the five children were all through looking little Faith over, Farmer John went to the door and called out "Topper! It's your turn to meet the new baby! Come on in here, Boy."

Barney ran up to the back door and watched the new puppy come in. And maybe Farmer John figured that the puppy was a little too feisty to be jumping around on the new baby, because he suddenly reached down and picked it up. He said, "You can come in and see the baby, Topper. But you're a little too short in the poop to be on the bed with the baby."

Barney and Topper looked at the baby. Their looks were priceless.

At the same time Barney's eyes were checking out baby Faith, little Topper was getting upset. He did not like being kept from the baby. Why was Farmer John holding him in his arms? Why couldn't he get on the bed with that little bundle that was lying there so quiet? It was almost his size. He could play with that new thing lying there in Molly's arms. But when he sniffed with his nose, that wiggly thing in the blanket did smell a little funny.

Topper kept his cool for a few minutes, and then began twisting and turning in Farmer John's arms. His intentions were clear. He wanted on the bed with the new baby. Molly and the kids had to laugh.

"Let me at it!" Topper howled. But Farmer John held him tight.

That did it. Molly smiled and then patted the bed beside her.

Farmer John's eyebrows shot up. He had a bit of a shocked look on his face. "Are you sure, Molly?" he asked. "He could jump in the baby's face and puts one of her eyes out. Anything could happen when you expose a brand spanking new baby to a little frisky puppy!"

"It's okay, John. It could be that we are witnessing something special here in this room. Think about it. Topper may be the one who will love and protect this new baby of ours. So I say put him on the bed so he can get used to her and used to her smell. We'll watch him close."

Molly's words were so positive that Farmer John did just as she said. He put Topper on the bed.

Well now. Do you know what that frisky little puppy did? He stood perfectly still for a minute or so and then crept slowly toward the baby. And all the while his little black nose was twitching.

Farmer John was flabbergasted.
He turned and looked at his children.
They were astonished, too.

Molly looked at the black-and-tan puppy and said, "Be very gentle, Topper. You must be careful with this little girl. You must learn to love and protect her."

The puppy was concentrating on Molly's facial expressions and her voice. He seemed to understand the words coming from her mouth.

But of course, being a puppy, that didn't hold his attention for long. After five or six seconds his little eyes went to the baby.

Faith's left arm moved a bit. She opened her eyes and looked at Topper. And even though it's a fact that babies cannot see very far when they are brand new, she was looking into the puppy's face. And if the muscles in her face were working, she would have smiled a big smile.

Farmer John suddenly realized that the new puppy and the new baby were going to be great friends. Yep.

"Everyone gather around the bed. Hurry, now," Joe's wife said as she raised a camera she had pulled out of her pocket. She took a picture of the entire family. And of course, it included two very proud daddies—Barney and Farmer John.

The next day, two men showed up and took the cheetah away.

That night, everyone felt safe. The cheetah was gone. Now if they had glanced at the window, they would have seen a big yellowish brown cat with black spots lurking outside. But they didn't. Besides, this house and everyone in it was safe. The man on guard was the main man, Ole Barney the Bear Killer.